The Big Basket

a story from Indonesia retold by
BARBARA BEVERIDGE

illustrated by Sheila Pearson

Chapter 1

Once there were three sisters. Their
parents had died, and the two older girls
looked after Little One, the youngest.
They were poor, but they grew fruit and
vegetables in their garden, and
sometimes they were able to catch fish
in the lake near their house. They helped
their neighbours in the fields in return
for some of the rice.

One day, Little One found a small bird under a bush in the garden. "Don't be frightened," she said. "I won't hurt you."

But the bird wasn't frightened. He seemed happy to let her pick him up. "Ke-ke-ko," he chirped. "Ke-ke-ko."

Little One made a cage from strips of cane, and the bird flew inside. She gave him some fruit and a few grains of rice. Then she hung his cage where she could talk to him while she worked in the garden.

When the older girls came home from the fields, the bird chirped, "Ke-ke-ko, ke-ke-ko," to welcome them. They were glad that their little sister had a pet to talk to while they were away.

Although the sisters were often hungry,
they always saved a little food for
Kekeko. Every morning he chirped to
thank them, and every evening he
welcomed them home.

$\mathcal{T}$hen one day something amazing happened.

"Take me out of my cage and put me in a basket," Kekeko said.

"Did you hear that?" said Little One. "Kekeko talked to us!"

"Take me out of my cage and put me in a basket," said Kekeko, "and you will never be hungry again."

"What do you think he means?" the sisters asked each other.

"Ke-ke-ko, ke-ke-ko. Put me in a basket," said the bird.

So the girls took him out of the cage and put him in a basket. They watched and waited, but nothing happened. They grew tired of waiting, and after the sun had gone down they went to bed.

The next morning when the sisters woke
up, they ran to the basket. It was full of
rice, and Kekeko was back in his cage.
The girls had never had so much rice to
eat. They cooked some and ate until they
could eat no more. There was still more
than enough rice for their evening meal.
They fed the bird and went off to work
in the fields and the garden.

When they came home in the evening, the bird welcomed them. "Ke-ke-ko, ke-ke-ko! Take me out of my cage and put me in a basket." This time they hurried to do what he asked.

The next morning and every morning after that, the girls found the basket full of rice and Kekeko back in his cage. Now they had more rice than they could eat themselves. They stored it in big baskets with lids on. They sold some of the rice at the market and used the money to buy other things they needed. And visitors were always welcome for a meal. They were amazed that the girls who had always been so poor now had so much rice to spare.

Chapter 3

Soon everyone in the village knew about the girls' good fortune. The news travelled to the next village, where their uncle lived. This uncle was a mean man. He had not visited them even once since their parents had died. Now he came hurrying to see them. "My dear nieces," he said, "I hope you are well."

"We are well, Uncle," they said.

"I'm sorry it's been such a long time since I saw you last," he said. "I've been so busy, you know."

"Yes, Uncle, we know you are a busy man," they said.

"But where did all this rice come from?" he asked, looking around their house. "From your neighbours? Your friends? Did you grow it all yourselves?"

"Oh no, Uncle," said Little One. "We used to be hungry all the time, but now our bird, Kekeko, gives us rice every day."

"But how can a bird do that?" asked their uncle.

"We just put him in a basket at night," said Little One, "and in the morning the basket is full of rice."

"Well, my dear nieces, I would very much like to borrow your bird for a few days," said their uncle.

The older girls looked at each other. "But, Uncle, we would miss Kekeko very much, and he would miss us too."

"Just till my rice baskets are full, you know. Then I will return him to you," said their uncle. "Surely you would like your uncle to share your good fortune."

What could the sisters do? "Very well, Uncle," they said. They watched as he put Kekeko in a small basket and carried him away. Would their uncle be kind to the bird? He had not been kind to them.

Chapter 4

A week later, the girls were still
waiting for their uncle to return the bird.
They missed his chirping, and soon they
would need more rice. They cleaned
Kekeko's cage and put in some rice and
fruit for him. Then they set out for their
uncle's village. It was a long way, but
they thought of their little bird. "He'll be
so happy to see us," said Little One. "I
hope Uncle has taken good care of him."

But when the girls got to their uncle's village, he was not pleased to see them. "What do you want?" he said angrily.

"Uncle, you did not return Kekeko," said the oldest sister. "We have come to get him."

"He's not here," said their uncle.

"But, Uncle, what have you done with him?"

"I ate him."

"Oh, Uncle," cried Little One, "you ate Kekeko! Why?"

"The stupid bird didn't give me any rice," their uncle shouted. "I put him in a basket every night and told him to give me rice, but every morning the basket was empty. Not one grain, do you hear? Not one!"

"Oh, Uncle, you should have been kind to him," said Little One.

"Well, I killed the stupid bird. Then I ate him, just to make sure he was gone."

The sisters burst into tears. "Now we'll never see Kekeko again," they cried.

Their uncle turned his back on them and walked into his house. "You can have his bones if you like," he called. "They're under the tamarind tree."

He laughed as he watched them looking for the tiny bones of their bird. They picked up all the bones they could find and wrapped them in a cloth.

Chapter
5

The sisters were full of sadness as they walked the long way home. Their uncle was as mean as ever, and their little bird was dead. He would never welcome them home again chirping "Ke-ke-ko, ke-ke-ko." And soon they would be poor again – there was not much rice left. Tomorrow they would have to go back to work in their neighbours' rice fields.

When they reached their house, the sisters put Kekeko's bones in the cage. Then they dug a hole in their garden and buried the cage, covering it over with earth and flowers. The older sisters hugged Little One, who could not stop crying, and they went to bed, too tired and sad to eat.

Next morning as the sun was rising, they
woke up and started to make breakfast
and tidy their house. Little One looked
out the door and across the garden. "Oh
… oh … come quickly!" she called.

They all ran to the place where Kekeko was buried. As the sun rose in the sky, it lit up a most wonderful tree that had grown in the night. The tree was covered with leaves and flowers of silk, all the colours of the rainbow.

Fruit made of red and yellow glass sparkled in the sun and made a musical sound in the breeze. No matter how many flowers or how much fruit the sisters picked, more grew to take their place.

They laughed and sang and danced around the tree. "We can sell the flowers and fruit at the market. We will never be poor again."

Then the three sisters became quiet as they remembered their little bird. "We'll never see Kekeko again," said the oldest sister, "but he is still helping us. We will never forget him."